Katie Woo

A Nervous Night

by Fran Manushkin

illustrated by Tammie Lyon

PICTURE WINDOW BOOKS

a capstone imprint

Katie Woo is published by Picture Window Books,
A Capstone Imprint
1710 Roe Crest Drive
North Mankato, Minnesota, MN 56003
www.capstonepub.com

Printed in the United States of America in Stevens Point, Wisconsin.
122014
008671R

Library of Congress Cataloging-in-Publication Data
Manushkin, Fran.
A nervous night / by Fran Manushkin; illustrated by Tammie Lyon.
p. cm. — (Katie Woo)
ISBN 978-1-4048-5725-4 (library binding)
ISBN 978-1-4048-6060-5 (paperback)
[1. Sleepovers—Fiction. 2. Grandparents—Fiction. 3. Chinese Americans—Fiction.]
I. Lyon, Tammie, ill. II. Title.
PZ7.M3195Ner 2010
[E]—dc22
2009030619

Summary: Katie is nervous about a sleepover at her grandparents' house.

Art Director: Kay Fraser
Graphic Designer: Emily Harris
Production Specialist: Michelle Biedscheid

Photo Credits
Fran Manushkin, pg. 26
Tammie Lyon, pg. 26

Table of Contents

Chapter 1
A **Sleepover**

Katie Woo was going to a sleepover at Grandma and Grandpa's house.

She packed her suitcase. Then she kissed her mom and dad goodbye.

Katie climbed into the car.
"I'm so glad you moved
close to me," she told her
grandparents. "Now I can
sleep over a lot!"

When Katie saw the house,
she smiled.

"It's a little house in a big
woods," she said.

"It's cozy," said Grandma.
"You'll see."

Katie put her suitcase in
the guest room.

It didn't look cozy at all.

The bed was too big, and

the walls were a yucky color.

"Come and plant some tomatoes with me," said Grandpa.

Outside, Katie dug holes and dropped tiny seeds in them.

"In the summer, we'll pick the tomatoes together," Grandpa promised.

Inside, Katie helped

Grandma make wontons.

"The next time you visit,"

said Grandma, "we'll make

noodle soup."

"This house is fun," Katie said.

"Indoors and out!" said Grandma. "From our porch we can see the sunset."

"And when you come in the summer," said Grandpa, "you will see shooting stars."

Chapter 2
The High Bed

"It's bath time!" called

Grandma.

"Hey," Katie said, "this

tub has legs. Are you sure it

won't walk away with me?"

"I'm sure," said Grandma.

"You never know," said

Katie.

After her bath, Katie put

on her pajamas.

"I don't like this bed,"

Katie decided. "It's too high.

What if I fall out?"

"This is your mother's old

bed," Grandma said. "She

never fell out."

"Really?" said Katie.

"Being up so high *does* make me feel like a princess."

"And our home is your castle," Grandma said with a smile.

"This castle
is a little spooky
right now," Katie
told Grandpa.

"Don't worry!"
he told her. "We have a
night-light."

"Yikes!" Katie yelled.

"There's a bear in my castle."

"That's just the shadow of

your mom's old teddy bear!"

said Grandpa.

"Right! I knew that!"

said Katie.

She grabbed the teddy

bear and hugged him tight.

Chapter 3
A Talk with Mom

"Would Princess Katie

like some cookies?" offered

Grandpa.

"I'd like to call Mom,"

Katie decided.

"Mom!" said Katie into the phone. "You forgot your teddy bear. Maybe I should come home with it now."

"That's okay," said her mom. "You can bring it back tomorrow."

"Katie," said Grandpa, "I wish you'd stay. I made your favorite — ginger cookies."

"And I will sing your mom's favorite lullabies," Grandma added.

Katie's mom
told her, "Nobody
sings lullabies
like Grandma!

I miss them — and
Grandpa's cookies too."

"All right!" Katie decided.
"I'll stay."

After cookies and milk,
Katie snuggled under the
covers.

"In the summer," she told
Grandma and Grandpa, "we
will eat tomatoes and make
noodles and see shooting stars!"

"I'm coming back — for sure!" Katie told the teddy bear.

And she dreamed of shooting stars all night.

About the Author

Fran Manushkin is the author of many popular picture books, including *How Mama Brought the Spring*; *Baby, Come Out!*; *Latkes and Applesauce: A Hanukkah Story*; and *The Tushy Book*. There is a real Katie Woo — she's Fran's great-niece — but she never gets in half the trouble of the Katie Woo in the books. Fran writes on her beloved Mac computer in New York City, without the help of her two naughty cats, Cookie and Goldy.

About the Illustrator

Tammie Lyon began her love for drawing at a young age while sitting at the kitchen table with her dad. She continued her love of art and eventually attended the Columbus College of Art and Design, where she earned a bachelors degree in fine art. After a brief career as a professional ballet dancer, she decided to devote herself full time to illustration. Today she lives with her husband, Lee, in Cincinnati, Ohio. Her dogs, Gus and Dudley, keep her company as she works in her studio.

Glossary

castle (KASS-uhl)—a large building often surrounded by a wall and a moat

favorite (FAY-vuh-rit)—the thing you like best

ginger (JIN-jur)—a spice to flavor cookies and other foods

guest (GEST)—someone who has been invited to visit or stay in another person's home

lullabies (LUHL-uh-byez)—gentle songs sung to help a child fall asleep

pajamas (puh-JAM-uhz)—clothing to sleep in

wontons (WAHN-tahns)—filled pockets of noodle dough; they are a common Chinese food

Discussion Questions

1. Katie was nervous at her grandparents' house. Why do you think she feels that way?

2. Have you ever slept over at someone's house? Where did you go? What did you do?

3. Think of a time you were nervous. What made you feel that way? What did you do to calm your nerves?

Writing Prompts

1. Katie's grandparents do special things like make wontons and plant tomatoes. What special things do you do with your grandparents or another special adult? Make a list of five things.

2. Katie sleeps in a high bed. Draw a picture of yourself sleeping in a high bed. Write a sentence to describe how it feels.

3. One of Katie's favorite treats is ginger cookies. What is your favorite treat? Write a paragraph to answer these questions: What do you like about it? Where do you get it? Where do you like to eat it?

Having **Fun**
with **Katie Woo**

In this book, Katie feels very nervous. Feelings, like being nervous, are interesting topics for poems. Try writing an acrostic poem that captures a feeling. In an acrostic poem, the first letters of each line of the poem combine to form a word. That word is the topic of your poem. So let's get started!

Write an Acrostic Poem!

1. Choose a feeling word, like happy, angry, or scared. We used the word nervous in our example.

2. Write your word going up and down. (See the example at right.) Each letter of the word will become the first letter of each line of your poem.

N
E
R
V
O
U
S

3. Now write the lines of your poem. With each line, describe something that reminds you of your feeling word, like in this nervous poem.

Noises that are creepy

Everyone looking at you

Roller coasters

Visiting the doctor

Owies that bleed

Unfamiliar people

Stormy nights

4. When you are done writing your poem, copy it neatly on a large piece of paper. Then draw pictures that illustrate it. Don't forget to share it with your friends and family!